Hey! You!
Gordon Goat!

by Ann Bryant and David Arumi

FRANKLIN WATTS
LONDON • SYDNEY

Gordon Goat lived in a big green field.

All day long, he munched on tasty green grass.

Gordon was happy.

But, one day, some men came from town.

They wanted to build houses

in the big green field.

"That digger will dig up my tasty green grass,"

Gordon said to himself.

He didn't like the men and the digger

in his field. So he set off to town to find

a new home.

Soon, Gordon came to a car park.

He was starting to feel hungry.

He looked around for something to eat.

"The tyres look tasty," he said to himself.

"I can munch on those all day long.

Gordon was about to start munching
when a lady shouted,
"Hey, you! What do you think you're doing?"
Gordon didn't like the lady so he ran away.
"I'll go and look for somewhere else to live,"
he said to himself.
"There must be somewhere with lots of food
for me."

Just down the road, Gordon came to

a sweet shop.

He could see jars and jars of sweets.

He was still hungry.

"Yum! They look tasty," he said.

"I can munch on those all day long.

This would be a good place to live."

But he'd hardly licked his lips

when a man started shouting at him.

"Hey, you! Get out of here!"

Gordon didn't like the man.

"It's time to go," he said.

"I'll look for somewhere else to live."

Next, Gordon came to a playground.

He was very hungry now.

He could see lots of bins.

"They might have something for me to eat," he said to himself.

He was just about to jump over the fence into the playground, when a man pointed to a notice.

"Hey, you!" he shouted. "Can't you read?"

NO GOATS

Gordon started to run away
but then he spotted something interesting
on the other side of the road.

It was a big red bus full of people.

"They might have something for me to eat," Gordon said.

"And this bus would be a good place for me to live."

10

He jumped onto the bus and started
to look in people's bags.
"Hey, you! Go away!" everyone shouted
and they shooed Gordon off the bus.

sat on the pavement.

... sad.

Would he ever find a home

with lots of food to eat?

He saw a sign that made his eyes light up.

BILL'S BAKERY

"This shop would be a good home for me,"
Gordon said.

"I could munch on these all day long."

He was looking at the cakes

when a man shouted,

"Hey, you! Get out of my shop!"

15

Gordon was scared. Why was everyone cross
with him? A big tear rolled down
his face and onto a lady's shoe.
The lady smiled at him.
"Don't worry," she said quietly.
"I will help you. Then you can help me."

"This is my goat," the lady said to the baker. "We came into the shop to look for a cake for our tea. But I can see that you do not like goats in your shop. We will go and get our cakes in another shop."

Gordon went home with the lady.
"I need some help with my garden,"
she smiled. "I think you can help me."
So Gordon found a good place to live
and he could munch on
lots of tasty green grass.

Story order

Look at these 5 pictures and captions.
Put the pictures in the right order
to retell the story.

1

The lady wanted to help Gordon.

2

Gordon was chased out of the sweet shop.

3

A digger came to Gordon's field.

4

Gordon ate the lady's grass.

5

Gordon saw a bakery.

Independent Reading

This series is designed to provide an opportunity for your child to read on their own. These notes are written for you to help your child choose a book and to read it independently.

In school, your child's teacher will often be using reading books which have been banded to support the process of learning to read. Use the book band colour your child is reading in school to help you make a good choice. *Hey, You! Gordon Goat!* is a good choice for children reading at Purple Band in their classroom to read independently.

The aim of independent reading is to read this book with ease, so that your child enjoys the story and relates it to their own experiences.

About the book

When a digger comes to dig up the field, Gordon the Goat needs to find a new home. But he is unwelcome wherever he goes. Then a kind lady offers to help him, and he helps her in return by munching the grass in her garden.

Before reading

Help your child to learn how to make good choices by asking: "Why did you choose this book? Why do you think you will enjoy it?" Look at the cover together and ask: "What do you think the story will be about?" Ask your child to think of what they already know about the story context. Then ask your child to read the title aloud. Ask: "Do you think people are being friendly when they say, 'Hey, You!'?" Remind your child that they can sound out the letters to make a word if they get stuck.

Decide together whether your child will read the story independently or read it aloud to you.

During reading

Remind your child of what they know and what they can do independently. If reading aloud, support your child if they hesitate or ask for help by telling the word. If reading to themselves, remind your child that they can come and ask for your help if stuck.

After reading

Support comprehension by asking your child to tell you about the story. Use the story order puzzle to encourage your child to retell the story in the right sequence, in their own words. The correct sequence can be found on the next page.

Help your child think about the messages in the book that go beyond the story and ask: "Why do you think Gordon was not welcome in the town? Why was he welcome in the garden at the end of the story?"

Give your child a chance to respond to the story: "Have you ever helped someone and then that person has helped you in return?"

Extending learning

Help your child predict other possible outcomes of the story by asking: "If Gordon had not met the lady at the bakery, can you think of any other places where he might have found a good home?"

In the classroom, your child's teacher may be teaching different kinds of sentences. There are many examples in this book that you could look at with your child, including statements, commands and questions. Find these together and point out how the end punctuation can help us decide what kind of sentence it is.

Franklin Watts
First published in Great Britain in 2018
by The Watts Publishing Group

Series Editors: Jackie Hamley and Melanie Palmer
Series Advisors: Dr Sue Bodman and Glen Franklin
Series Designer: Peter Scoulding

A CIP catalogue record for this book is
available from the British Library.

ISBN 978 1 4451 6227 0 (hbk)
ISBN 978 1 4451 6229 4 (pbk)
ISBN 978 1 4451 6228 7 (library ebook)

Printed in China

Franklin Watts
An imprint of
Hachette Children's Group
Part of The Watts Publishing Group
Carmelite House
50 Victoria Embankment
London EC4Y 0DZ

An Hachette UK Company
www.hachette.co.uk

www.franklinwatts.co.uk

Answer to Story order: 3, 2, 5, 1, 4

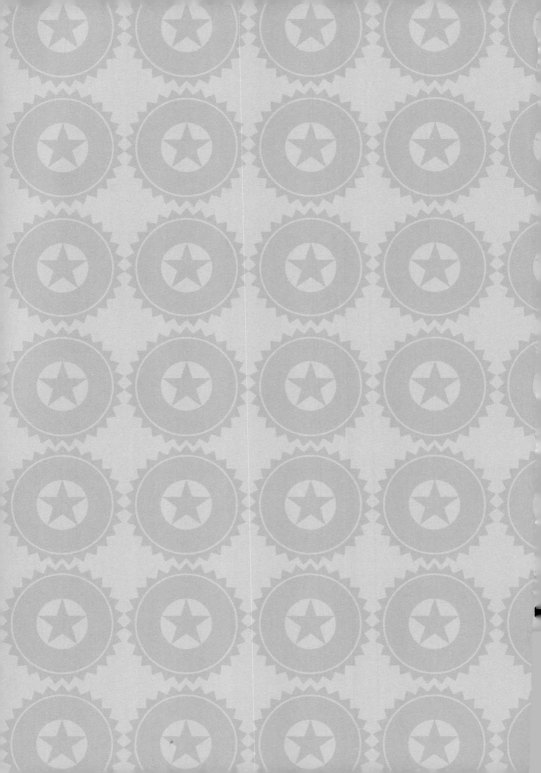